A FEW MORE RULES

DOROTHY F. SHAW

Red Queen
Publications

PRAISE FOR DOROTHY F. SHAW

"*Unworthy Heart* reminded me of what I love about the romance genre."—The Book Tart

"*Unworthy Heart* by Dorothy F. Shaw made me think, made my heart happy, made me tear up and made me sigh in happiness. Shaw combines heat with heart almost flawlessly. I cannot wait for the follow-up books in this series."—Romance Novel News

"I fell in love with the series from book one…Grab your copy and buckle up for the ride. Dorothy Shaw doesn't do anything halfway."—Beyond the Valley of the Books on *Defensive Heart*

"Holy smokes, can Dorothy Shaw write a freaking awesome sex scene…"—Wicked Good Reads on *Defensive Heart*

"*Defensive Heart* by Dorothy F. Shaw is a good read which gives credence to the statement that opposites do attract."—Harlequin Junkie

"Even though there is plenty of sex in *Shattered Heart*, the author does not neglect the storyline at all – packing it full of romance, danger, trauma, healing, laughs, and the Donnelly family."—Crystal's Many Reviewers

"*Shattered Heart* is an emotional tear-jerker of a romance that had me reaching for the tissues on more than one occasion."—Romance Novel News

"Wow! What a sexy, steamy story that kept me reading from the first page."—Crystal's Many Reviewers on *Stripped Bounty*

"If you are into vanilla, forget this book! Characters larger than life and sex to die for. Dorothy F. Shaw painted a canvas that is both intriguing and close to hardcore."—Amazon Reviewer on *Stripped Bounty*

"Epic story! Rosie and Badger are amazing characters that pull you into the story. The sex is HOT and the ending is perfect!"—Book Addicts PR on *Stripped Bounty*

"I was blown away by how easily the story was told by Dorothy F. Shaw"—CeeriJays Smexy HotReads on *A Few More Rules*

"*A Few More Rules* (a femdom novella) is a super-hot romance that sets the foundation well for a probable HEA between Rig and Beth. This story is a winner."—Romance Novel News

"WOW!!! This erotic, sensual short story will have you panting for more! These two beauties are more than fang bangers. The dark world of lust and sex will feed any appetite you desire."—Bookaholic and More Blog on *Playtime*

"I like books that grab my attention so much that I read a line and end up gasping or commenting out loud... and this one did just that - a few times! I'll definitely be reading it again."—Goodreads Reviewer on *Playtime*

"True to Dorothy Shaw's form, *Avoiding the Badge* is full of everything I love about her writing."—Amanda at Wicked Good Reads

"I liked the way the author brought about the truths that they had been keeping from each other, and I really enjoyed the steps that the two characters took in order to overcome the troubles in their path."—Amazon reviewer on *Avoiding the Badge*

"*Redeeming the Badge* is a second chance romance that is hot as Hades and with a backstory that will twist your heartstrings." —Amazon Reviewer

"This is a tale of love and heartache, dealing with some tough issues such as infertility, endometriosis, and miscarriage. It will tear at your heartstrings and make you believe in true love." —Amazon Reviewer on *Redeeming the Badge*

"Jeff and Tish are a good couple with incredible chemistry that makes you jealous. I can't recommend this series enough." —Amazon Reviewer on *Trusting the Badge*

"*Trusting the Badge* is a quick read for readers who enjoy a focus on relationship building, characters with tragic backstories, and some steamy moments." —Amazon Reviewer

"It was written in a way that I got very emotional reading it, most books don't make me cry. This one did."—Amazon reviewer on *Jaded Heart*

"As usual, Shaw creates characters that can be hard to like. Garrett is not easy to connect to. He treats Angie like crap, but Angie keeps fighting for them. Their flameout moment is painful to read about but very necessary. Garrett has to deal with his past, which he has been avoiding for years and years. With all of this, I still couldn't put the book down."—Romance Novel News on *Jaded Heart*

A Few More Rules

Sometimes getting on your knees leads down a path of salvation…and happily ever after.

Finding "the one" is never easy for anybody, but Bethany Carlson hasn't even bothered looking for hers. Especially since finding a true submissive male is something that only exists in her deepest fantasies. That is until she meets Rig.

Rig Jenkins, a former college football hopeful turned strip club bouncer, is out for a night to escape the grind of daily life… and the past he can never quite forget. He isn't looking for anyone or anything, but when he catches a glimpse of Bethany, and her girl-next-door appearance, he can't help but want to know more.

Bethany knows immediately that Rig is the sort of man she could only dream of—strong, submissive and meant only for her. But is Rig strong enough to let her lead him to the place he was always meant to be?

DEDICATION

*For all the women who need to be in control, and for the men who are
strong enough to beg them to be...*

ACKNOWLEDGMENTS

Thank you to my sweet Bethany, for allowing me the use of your name and image for the inspiration of the heroine. She's not you, of course, and you are the furthest thing from a female Dominant, but that's why it's called fiction! Much love, honey.

A big thank you to author Sidda Lee Rain! As usual, Momma, you carry me through as my writing sprint partner in crime! I got nothing but naked love for you!

Super big thank you to author Megan Hart for beta reading this little novella and letting me know it didn't suck. And also the title suggestion. My writing slump was long and deep, and I'm grateful it's over. You're always reminding me that my writing doesn't suck…and this go-round, I really needed to hear it. And for that, I am eternally in your debt. Love you, Bebe!

CHAPTER ONE

"Be right with you!"

Rig Jenkins glanced to his right as a petite bar waitress brushed by him in such a rush the only thing he caught a glimpse of was her back. And also her bottom—and a mighty fine glimpse it was. As Rig took his seat on a stool at the bar, he also took a little more time to behold her backside before she turned and ran off to another table.

"What can I get you?"

Rig turned and faced the tall brunette, wearing more makeup than he preferred to see on women, behind the bar. Clearing his throat, he glanced over the booze lining the shelves behind her. Whiskey and Bourbon was definitely a thing in this place. There had to be at least a hundred and fifty-plus different kinds. A good mix of craft and domestic beer on tap, too. He smiled at the brunette. "Bear with me, ma'am. 'Lotta choices."

She smiled, her glossy red lips shining in the overhead spotlights. "Craving anything specific?"

Rig rubbed his palms together. He was craving plenty, but what that was exactly, he wasn't about to get into with her.

"Guessing I'll keep it simple tonight. Shot of Jack and a Coors Light bottle, please?"

She winked. "Coming right up."

As she went to work filling his order, Rig glanced around the table area in search of the petite waitress who'd rushed past him not three minutes earlier. She was off in the far corner, nodding—a soft smile on her face, as a guy sporting a big belly and cowboy hat talked to her. Though Rig could only see her profile, it was obvious she was a real pretty girl.

"Here you go."

Rig turned his attention to the shot and beer now sitting before him on the polished wood bar top. And then the smiling brunette. She was pretty, too, but more on the too high maintenance side of the scale, which added up to definitely not his type of pretty. He nodded and lifted the shot. "Thank you, ma'am."

"So polite." She tipped her head to one side and tucked a lock of her long hair behind an ear. "Name's Connie. If you need anything else…anything at all, don't hesitate to holler."

Her eyes went soft and all doe-eyed. The silvery shadow coating her eyelids sparkled from the overhead lights as she made a show of blinking, all slow and alluring.

Rig smirked and tossed the shot back. Yep, all done up and definitely not his type. And even though he saw tits and ass on a daily basis working security at Deuce's Cabaret, Connie's cleavage pushed up from the tight leather vest she wore was nothing to shake a stick at.

They just weren't a pair he'd choose to shake *his* stick at.

WITH A SMILE ON HER FACE, Bethany Carlson shifted her hips side to side, listening to one of the regulars prattle on about something with his work, and people not doing their jobs, and yada-yada, blah, blah…only he could save the day because of how smart he was.

The band was gearing up to start, and as the guy paused in his—look at me, I'm just so amazing—story to sip his drink, Bethany took it as her cue to get moving. "You need another, Tom?"

"Absolutely!" He smiled, his full, round face appearing rounder.

She didn't want to be rude, truly. She was raised better than that. Instead, she smiled, she nodded and did her best to appear interested while at the same time figuring out a way to move along and tend to her other customers. Smile, nod. Smile, nod…rinse, lather, repeat. "Coming right up!"

On her way back to the server station located at the end of the bar, another customer snagged her arm and asked for a refill and a menu. Then another requested their tab—

Thursday night at The Whiskey Barrel. Ladies night and always busy. But busy was good for Bethany's wallet. Plus, the crowd favorite, a local band called Zona Road, provided a full playlist of country cover songs and did one hell of a job belting them out.

The patrons, a mix of old and young country danced until their hearts were content on the small dance floor, and Bethany navigated in and around them and the others surrounding the tables, keeping everyone's drink card full.

After calling out her order to Connie, she closed out the tab for the customer who'd asked, pulled the pen she'd stuck in the bun at the back of her head free, and laid it in the bill-folder ready for signing. Stepping away, she delivered it to where it needed to go, grabbed a couple of empties off the table, promised another bill to a customer and rushed back to the bar.

Hustling from one customer to the next, making sure they all had what they needed, was the name of the game. Though it kept the tips rolling in, which is what she needed most, a bonus benefit was it also helped keep her ass at the size she much preferred it to be, too.

With a menu tucked under one arm, the new bill-folder under the other and drinks in both hands, Bethany spun to head off and make her deliveries— And collided with a rather large patron passing in front of her.

"Shoot!" The trickle of cold liquid slid down her hands and forearms, and she instinctively shot her hips back in attempt to keep the spillage from hitting her bare legs.

The guy grabbed her upper arm. "Oh, damn. You okay?"

"Yeah. All good, just need a towel." She glanced up, ready to reassure him with an easy smile…and lost her breath. *My, oh my.* Before she realized what was happening, he'd snagged a bar towel from the stack next to the server station, took one of the drinks from her hand, and began cleaning her up.

Bethany stood dumbstruck, taking in his features. *My word, he's beautiful.* And tall, so tall. The rough rub of the stiff cotton towel on her forearm snapped her out of her momentary drooling-over-a-hot-guy stupor, and she slipped the rag from his hand. "Thank you, I'm okay."

He stuck his free hand in his pocket and shrugged. "I'm real sorry for plowing into you like that, ma'am."

"No harm—a tremor ran through her—done." *Did he… ma'am?* The sound of the word, in his deep tone of voice and slight southern accent, had heat radiating from her lower abdomen through her limbs.

Working as a bar waitress these past couple of years, Bethany had been addressed a thousand different ways. Honey, baby, sweetheart, miss, dear, sweetie, even cutie…but never ma'am. Apparently, "ma'am" birthed a fire inside her so hot it turned her blood to burning lava unlike anything ever had before.

Wow, she more than liked, if not loved, the sensations, as well as the mental and emotional responses running rampant through every inch of her body, but hell, if she had any idea why she was reacting this way.

In an effort to distract herself, even if only a little, Bethany finished the cleanup job. When she was done, she tossed the towel aside and did her best to put a lid on the vibrations still ping-ponging around her insides. She cleared her throat in order to talk and not sound like a complete doofus. "I'll take that drink back now."

With a slight shake of his head and a sexy smile arching his too-perfect lips, he glanced away from her for a heartbeat and then met her gaze again. "Yes, ma'am."

Heat rose up Bethany's neck and face, and she thought for sure she was the color of a bright red apple. *Good grief.* He stepped closer, and the scent of clean soap filled her lungs… and her knees went loose.

The warmth radiating off his big, muscular body surrounded her, and every inch of her skin tingled in response. And then a shiver raced down her spine. Unable to stop herself, Bethany tilted her head back to keep eye contact and let out a sigh. *Gorgeous smile…*

The urge to tell him to get on his knees plowed through Bethany's brain with a force so severe she sucked in a breath.

Before the words had a chance to manifest, the feel of the cool glass hit her palm, and Bethany tore her gaze away long enough to grasp the drink in her hand so she didn't drop it. Catching his eyes again, she couldn't stop a smile from arching her lips—not that she wanted to stop it, though. "Thanks." She shrugged as relief spilled through her that she hadn't blurted out a command she'd never in her life given before. "Gotta go deliver these."

Another moment passed, the tension between them thick as molasses, before he nodded and stepped aside. Instantly, Bethany felt the absence of his big body as if he'd been wrapped around her, but suddenly let her go and pulled away.

An almost feral craving clawed at her insides to have the heat of him around her again.

Which was crazy!

Aside from when he grabbed her arm, their bodies hadn't even touched!

Stupid crazy!

Frowning at the unexpected feeling of loss inching along her skin and settling in her stomach like a block of ice, she stepped away and headed toward her waiting customers. It wasn't like she didn't see good-looking guys on a regular basis. She saw them all the time.

Bars were full of them. And country bars had them in spades, for sure. She never engaged with them, though. Never flirted or lingered or was even interested. What on earth could be so different about this one? Why him?

Bethany was baffled, except…good grief, his smile! The man's smile took his already good looks and sent them right off the charts. The light was dim in the bar, but not dim enough where she couldn't see the color of his eyes. They were blue and gorgeous. Close-cropped, brown hair, chiseled jawline. Full lips. Over six feet tall and definitely muscular—as in washboard abs kind of muscular. She didn't need to see beneath his t-shirt and flannel to know that was a fact. The boy was straight-up fine—no doubt about it.

But her sudden attraction to him was more than all of those things combined. Question was, did she want to find out how much more?

CHAPTER TWO

RIG WATCHED THE EPITOME OF THE PERFECT GIRL-NEXT-DOOR walk away from him, and once again, he admired the incredible view of her behind in denim short shorts. Except this time, he also took the opportunity to check out her silky legs. His jeans got a whole lot tighter in the fly area, and his palms ached to know if her skin felt as soft as it looked.

She wore very little makeup, if any at all, which he *loved*. Her hair was pulled into a thick bun positioned low at the base of her head. She wore a flannel shirt, tied into a knot at her waist and some sort of barely there lace tank top underneath it. And cowgirl boots, good God, boots! Rig ran his palm over his head. Damn, she was sexy.

He'd called her ma'am—no different from how he addressed all females he came in contact with. It was a respect thing his Momma and Daddy ensured he learned as a kid, but for some reason, when he said it to this girl, it felt way different.

The second the respectful term had passed his lips, her eyes had flared, a fire sparking in them. But then, almost immediately, as if he was connected to her in some mystical way, his body responded like she'd called him directly to her—and he followed the instinct, stepping as close as he could get.

God Almighty, when Rig touched her arm, and the heat of her skin passed through the thin flannel sleeve to his palm, his dick had gone rod hard. Even so, he knew on some sort of molecular level he'd been wrong to touch her without asking. When he let go, all he could think about was how much he wanted—no, *needed* to touch her again.

After she'd taken the bar rag from him to finish cleaning up the spill, he stuffed his hands in his pockets like a stupid, insecure teenager. He didn't trust himself, and looking like a fool was far better than touching her again without permission.

Truth be told, the way some of the world lacked respect for personal boundaries made Rig's stomach turn. No matter a person's gender, they didn't have the right to touch someone without their consent—another thing his parents had made sure he understood even as a small boy. Though his family wasn't perfect, without a doubt, his parents had raised him right.

Once he'd started getting older and having girlfriends, Rig never laid his hands on a woman without being invited to do so. But this instinctual pull, driving him to go to her, was something entirely different. Unable to process everything swirling around his head, Rig moved back to his seat at the bar and ordered another beer.

An idea niggled at the back of his mind, just out of reach. Rig sipped from the beer bottle and watched his tiny waitress move about the bar as the idea—which had started as little and ridiculous—grew into something so big and undeniable there was nothing to do but throw all the doors and windows open and face it.

Yes, the need for her to give him permission was rooted in respecting her rights for personal space and as a human being…but more than all of that combined, it had everything to do with simply *pleasing* her *and* gaining her approval.

Rig knew the same as he knew his own name, if she asked him to go to his knees, even right there in front of an entire bar full of people, he'd do it. He'd crawl to her if it were what she wanted. He'd kiss her petite little cowboy-booted feet, too. And not because it was some demeaning or humiliating act he'd get off on.

No. Doing it for her and *only* her didn't feel demeaning or humiliating. It felt liberating. It felt like what she wanted or needed was the only thing that mattered, and the power of being the one to give her *any and all* things pulsed through him in time with his heartbeat. As if it was what he was meant to do…

But beneath all of it, flowing like a raging river, was a deep, primal *need* to please her. And he didn't even know her name.

Where the fuck all these unusual emotional and sexual realizations—at least unusual for him—were coming from, Rig had no clue. He only knew they were right and true.

With his thoughts boomeranging around his head like speeding bullets, Rig signaled the bartender for another shot. After he'd swallowed the golden, brown liquid, and the burn traveled from his throat to his belly, he tried to wrap some logic around what he was feeling and what this could be saying about who he was as a person.

He wasn't a weak guy. He didn't let anyone lead him around by his nose…or his dick, for that matter. Although the thought of this little lady taking a hold of his cock only made things get tighter behind his zipper.

"You stare any harder, you might actually burn a hole in her ass with your eyes."

Rig whipped his head around to find the bartender, Connie, wiping down the bar surface in front of him. He smirked. "That obvious?"

She rolled her eyes. "Beyond obvious. You're welcome to keep at it, but you're wasting your time. Bethany doesn't ever mess with the customers."

"That feels a whole lot like a challenge. Or are you jealous?" Rig tipped his beer back for a swallow.

Connie dipped her chin and raised a brow. "Honey, please. I have no reason to be jealous of Bethany."

Rig watched her walk away and couldn't help but chuckle. He'd been half-teasing with the "jealous" question. But clearly, the woman wasn't used to anyone besides her getting attention. However, the idea that she could be arrogant or self-centered enough to believe Bethany—Jesus, what a perfect name for her—wasn't pretty or beautiful enough to gain attention from a man, made Connie look like an ugly hag to him.

Before he'd even been face-to-face with Bethany, Rig could see she was pretty. But watching her for the last twenty minutes or so, as she did her job waiting on the patrons in the bar, he'd decided she was beyond beautiful.

Her beauty was in the way she smiled at her customers. The way she stopped and gave them her full attention as they talked to her. But also, it was evident in how they treated her. It was obvious, by observing the patrons who were familiar with her, that she was regarded as someone with a genuine heart. Their faces would change, their expressions going soft when they spoke to her.

Beauty wasn't only skin deep, for sure. What made a person pretty, or beautiful even, was what their heart and character was made of. So far, Bethany was proving his line of thinking to be correct. All Rig had to figure out now was how he was going to earn the privilege of her attention.

In more ways than just her customer.

———

Bethany cleared a table of the empties and tried for all it was worth not to glance over at the bar for the eight-hundredth-millionth time in the last few hours. That freaking gorgeous, tall and muscular country boy was still sitting there. Bottle of beer and shot glass in front of him.

On occasion, he got up and went to the men's room and then came back to his stool. But aside from that, he hadn't talked to anyone. Hadn't danced with anyone. Amazingly, he'd barely paid Connie any mind either—from what Bethany could tell anyway.

What *he had* done was watch Bethany.

All.

Night.

Long.

When she caught his eyes, he would nod at her. Some-times, he would smile. Other times, he would simply stare at her. It wasn't creepy or stalkerish. On the contrary, it was like he was waiting for something.

Waiting for her, maybe… The expression on his face was one of patience and contentment. As if he would sit there until she told him to go, or stay, or do anything she wanted.

Although Bethany didn't do one-night stands, ever, the idea of taking him to her home, to her bed and having him do whatever she requested had lust tightening her stomach and shooting like a bolt of lightning to her clit. For God's sake, her panties had been wet the better part of the night because of him.

Back at the server station—and only a mere few feet away from where he sat—Bethany's skin grew tingly, and her lower abdomen clenched in a knot. She blew out a breath, trying to expel some of the tension pulsing inside her as she tossed the empty beer bottles in the trash before lining the dirty glasses up for the bar back to wash.

Life hadn't been full of sexual partners; she'd only been with a few men. In fact, Bethany could count them all on one hand, with fingers to spare, including her high school boyfriend. But none of them had lit a fire inside her like this stranger was doing—by simply sitting there.

In the last year or so, romance books had been the key to unlocking desires inside of Bethany she'd had no idea were there. To some, it was a completely taboo thing, somewhere far across the line of kinky.

The idea of being the dominant one, a female Dom—the one who called the shots and made the rules, had her searching for that one perfect man.

A man who was willing to get on his knees for her and only her.

Although she was certain the kinky kind of sex where she got to be the one in charge could never be found, at the age of twenty-three, Bethany had also given up on finding the perfect, emotional connection she'd dreamed of having. That type of chemistry was only something that existed in fiction.

In truth, she'd never even bothered to look for it. And for all she knew, what she was feeling right then only meant she was horny. It *had* been a while since she'd had sex. Lust could screw with the brain and make a person feel things that weren't real, all in the name of a much needed orgasm.

"Ma'am?"

Bethany froze as a ripple of pure lust rushed through her body, filling her from head to toe. The feeling rocked her to the core, and she had to close her eyes, grip the edge of the counter and remind herself to breathe. When she felt she'd composed herself enough, she raised her eyes and found his gaze instantly.

He'd moved to the end of the bar, right next to the server station. Bethany swallowed, and felt something else rise inside her she wasn't sure how to label. Strength, dominance, control? She wasn't sure, but she let it lead her. Bethany stepped around the edge of the bar and stood in front of him. "Tell me your name."

He inclined his head. "Name's Rig, ma'am."

Her stomach clenched, and her clit pulsed. Bethany stifled a moan and schooled her features. Could she orgasm from hearing him call her ma'am? Was that even a thing? "Rig? That's an interesting name."

"Grew up on a farm; friends gave it to me. And then—"

Bethany watched as he drew in a deep breath, his big chest expanding with the action, his tall frame tightening, but not in a good way. Obviously, she'd hit a nerve and with only one single question…or was it from the answer he'd given? Only one way to find out. "…And then, what?"

His expression darkened. "Then with football…it stuck."

With no idea where this was going, she pressed on. "Football, hmm? What position do you play?"

He ran his palm along the back of his neck, his brow furrowed, and a corner of his lip dipped into a frown. "Don't play anymore, but quarterback."

Bethany ached to smooth away the distress coating his beautiful features. Yet, curiosity tickled at the edges of her mind. She needed to know more. Plus, she was no fool. Clearly, the conversation served as an excellent distraction since what she wanted to do was climb his tall body like a cat in heat. "Why don't you play anymore?"

He stuffed his hands in his pockets and shrugged, his expression now tired, almost defeated. "Just lucky, I guess."

Apparently, yes. A sensitive nerve for sure, and she'd knocked on the one door he didn't care to have opened where the topic was hiding out. Along with it, sharing space behind a locked emotional door was a boatload of pain, and Lord knew what else. Considering all of this, then why tell her anything at all? Bethany frowned and tilted her head to the side as the need to understand, as well as ease his pain, coated her insides. "Doesn't sound so lucky to me, but how about we talk more about that later?"

"Whatever you want, ma'am."

She drew in a deep breath. *Whatever she…* Good grief, did the man have *any* idea of how he was affecting her? "What's your real name?"

"Colby Jenkins." He held out his hand. "May I know yours?"

As she placed her hand in his, Bethany closed her eyes, and the electric current she expected would be there passed between them, flowing through her entire body…and this time, as her clit pulsed in time with her heart, she swore she actually *did* have an orgasm. Opening her eyes, she leveled her gaze on him. "Bethany Carlson. Pleasure to meet you."

"Pleasure's all mine." A broad smile spread across his mouth, revealing a set of perfect teeth.

Colby stroked his thumb over the top of Bethany's hand, and another shock blasted through her. She bit her bottom lip as more moisture coated her panties. Oh, dear. This was happening.

The cool breeze of relief mixed with satisfaction filled her mind, and she let her breath out as if she'd been holding it in forever.

Inching closer, she tipped her head back to gaze up at him. "Colby, you've been here nearly all night, but you haven't talked to anyone. Why is that?"

"I'm waiting for you."

She glanced down at their linked hands. "For me?"

"Yes, ma'am. To—" He shook his head and then closed his eyes. A moment later, he continued. "For you to tell me what it is you need."

Moving closer, Bethany ran the palm of her free hand up his bicep. "What then?"

"Then I'll set to giving you exactly what it is you need."

His gaze bore into Bethany's, and she felt everything inside her go still. Everything but her heart, which pounded hard enough that her skin throbbed right along with it. "What if what I need is for you to go home and shower? Then, come back here an hour after closing and meet me in the back parking lot. Would you do it?"

His bicep flexed under her grip. At the same time, a muscle in the side of his chiseled jaw jumped. "Yes."

Closing the distance between their bodies, Bethany rose on tiptoe and placed her lips at the side of his ear. "That was an easy one." She felt his free hand graze her hip, but then it was gone—so fast, she almost thought she imagined it. But she knew she hadn't. *Interesting.* "Are you waiting for permission to touch me, Colby?"

His breath came out of him in a rush. "Please, yes. May I?"

"May you, what?" As she whispered close to his ear, his body shuddered against hers. Heady waves of lust and power filled her stomach, making it tighten in response. Bethany's clit pulsed, and her cunt clenched, aching to be filled.

The sexual tension boiling inside her was so out of control that if he slid his big thigh between her legs and gave even the barest pressure against her core, she'd orgasm.

"Please, ma'am, may I touch you?"

Bethany gripped his arm, digging her fingertips into the fabric of his flannel shirt. "Yes, but not right now. You'll wait until later. For now, go do as I asked."

Another breath rushed out of him, and his body sagged against hers.

With every inch of Bethany's being, she wanted to feel this man's hands on her skin. With every fiber of her soul, she wanted to feel his body naked against hers. She wanted to taste him. She wanted to see his eyes when she let him slide between her legs.

Bethany wanted…all of it and more.

But not yet.

CHAPTER THREE

"Wʜᴀᴛ *ɪɴ* ᴛʜᴇ ғᴜᴄᴋ'ᴍ I ᴅᴏɪɴɢ?" Rᴏᴜɢʜʟʏ ᴀɴ ʜᴏᴜʀ ᴀɴᴅ thirty minutes after he'd left the bar, Rig stood in the back parking lot of the bar waiting for Bethany—as she'd asked him to do.

He was starting to question if his sanity was still intact. Actually, his list of "what the fuck moments" was growing by the minute. Ever since he'd laid eyes on the woman—several hours ago—all he could think about was her and what she needed from him.

The dynamic between them was different for him. Not that he was some sort of dominant, but for sure, he was no submissive. At least he hadn't ever been before. Never in his life had he felt a desire to take direction from a woman.

But that little girl had a thing about her, an air, as people called it. Whatever it was, it felt like he'd been punched in the stomach whenever he got near her.

Earlier, as he was trying to keep his shit together because he was close to her, she asked him about his nickname. No big deal—not something he had a problem sharing. A home-grown farm boy from Arkansas…built like a Mack Truck, a big rig.

But then, having no idea why, he went and mentioned football. Worse, he wanted to tell her about all of it—the whole tragic sob story.

For fuck's sake, Rig wanted to lay his head in her lap and cry like some weak little baby…while, at the same time, his dick was rock hard and aching to be inside her sweet cunt. Talk about a drastic conflict of feelings!

God help him, her pussy was probably tighter than a vice. He bet she tasted sweet as honey, too. When he'd showered— as she'd told him to do—he had no choice but to jack off to relieve some of the pressure. He'd come so hard, spurting all over the shower wall, that he'd seen spots.

After he'd toweled off and his cock was only half erect, it occurred to him she hadn't given him permission to stroke himself *or* to come. Almost immediately, before he'd even hung the towel up the dry, his dick had gone steel-hard again.

Leaning against the tailgate of his truck, Rig blew out a breath and adjusted his *still* erect cock behind his zipper. Even now, he was wondering if she was going to punish him for it. Jesus, a new item for page two of the "what the fuck moments." Never in his life had he had thoughts of a woman punishing him.

It was *his* damn dick. He'd stroke it if he wanted. As much as he wanted. Any time he wanted. But she hadn't— "Oh, for fuck's sake!"

"I see you did as I asked."

The soft tone of her voice arrowed straight to his balls, and Rig almost fell to his knees. Trying hard to maintain some level of calm in front of her, he gazed off into the distance like this was all no big deal, and he was chock-full of laid-back and calm.

But inside, his blood was boiling in his veins, and the desire to go to her and bury his hands and face in her hair was suffocating him. *Get a grip!* Okay, dammit. *Breathe.* Yeah, he was cool. *Breathe*. He was fine. All good. Rig turned his focus to her. "Yes, ma'am."

With a blank expression on her face, as if this play between them was all in his head, she nodded and brushed a few windblown stray hairs away from her eyes. "Your truck, I assume?"

Panic raced through Rig, replacing the false confidence he'd fooled himself into thinking he possessed. Shit! She didn't look happy. She didn't look pleased. *Shiiiit*! The urge to redeem himself, to adjust, or somehow fix it, had his skin tightening and his rib cage compressing his lungs. "Yes."

"I'm right over there in the blue Honda…" She pointed in the direction of her vehicle. "Follow me."

Without a thought, Rig moved to her side and held out his elbow. "If it's okay, I'll see you safely to your car."

She glanced down at his arm, then back to his face. "It's not necessary, but if it's important to you, I'll let you."

"Please." When she slid her small hand into the crook of his arm, Rig's body ignited into flames. "Thank you, ma'am."

The walk to her car took no more than a minute, but for the entire sixty seconds she was close to his body, Rig felt like he'd died and gone to heaven. They were barely touching, and it didn't matter. She was next to him. He was taking care of her. She trusted him to take care of her—even if it was only to get her safely across the dark parking lot.

Escorting women to their cars was something he did every night when on shift at the strip club. His entire job as a bouncer and security at Deuce's Cabaret was about protecting those dancers, and he never thought twice about it. It was easy for him and something he took pride in. His size and bulk helped, but his naturally protective instinct was the key. Probably why his direct boss, Badger, who was in charge of security, often called on Rig first.

But this moment with Bethany felt different than all of

that combined. They'd just met. He didn't know her, and she didn't know him. But that didn't matter one bit. A sense of peace filled his heart, spreading through his limbs. For the first time since his injury, Rig felt like he was doing exactly what he was meant to do.

He was right where he was supposed to be— Bethany was right where he was supposed to be.

After Rig delivered her to her car and ensured she was inside, and the engine started, he let the content feeling float through him. When he got in his truck to follow behind her, he had no idea what else was going to happen. He only knew he'd go wherever she wanted to lead him.

Again, peace filled his heart. It was wonderful. It was freeing. But it was also the most terrifying moment of his life.

And that included the moment years ago when he was lying injured on a college football field, praying his future wasn't over.

BETHANY TURNED up the radio as she drove home. *I believe In Love,* by the Dixie Chicks, was playing, and she sang along, keeping an eye on Colby in the rearview. She wasn't naive enough to think she'd found some sort of love at first sight with him.

Who knew if that even existed? Regardless, it was still up for debate whether or not a more than physical attraction at first sight could happen. Was it possible that maybe once in a lifetime, two total strangers could meet and be drawn to each other so magnetically, so immediately, they could do nothing but go with it? She couldn't be sure.

Even if it *were* possible, could it become love? Rolling her eyes, annoyance vibrated through Bethany at her ridiculousness, and she turned the radio off. "Don't be an idiot, Beth.

This isn't love. It's a one-night stand with a hot guy. So let's not get carried away into some made-up fantasy land, hmm?"

After she pulled into her apartment complex and parked her car in her assigned spot, Bethany waved Colby in the direction of the visitor spots and then waited on the sidewalk for him.

With deep anticipation pulsing through her, she watched his shadowed form step out of the pick-up, close the door and admired each of his long strides as he walked toward her. His body was perfection. Broad shoulders framed a muscular chest, leading to a V-shaped torso above a narrow and tight waist and hips. Strong, muscular thighs—heat rose in Bethany's body, her lower abdomen going tight with desire.

Her clit pulsed. Her hands shook. The power of what his body was capable of didn't escape her—especially since the man had been a football player. He could physically hurt her if he wanted, she was sure. But Bethany was equally as sure he wouldn't.

In addition, she knew, with absolute certainty, that Colby "Rig" Jenkins would do whatever it was she wanted or needed him to do.

He stopped in front of her, his hands loose at his sides. But the tension he carried in his body rolled off him in thick, heavy waves. He was trying to hide it, she could tell. Or, it could merely be sexual tension. Though, based on how he'd reacted earlier when they were first talking, Bethany had the feeling it was something deeper.

The desire to pull down the walls he'd built to hide whatever it was inside him was equally as strong as the desire to feel his naked body against hers. As if she'd seen it firsthand, she could feel a darkness inside his heart, and Bethany wanted to unleash it.

She wanted to see what he was holding onto for dear life —and why. Dangerous or not, she wanted to draw all of it out of him while he was pounding between her parted thighs.

Gazing up at him, Bethany placed her hand on his chest and felt his beating heart beneath her palm. "You ready for this?"

He drew in a deep breath. "I think so, yes."

Bethany nodded, took his hand and led him to her apartment door in silence. She handed him the keys, and he unlocked the door and pushed it open. After entering her small one-bedroom unit, Bethany set her things down on the countertop bar just past the kitchen entryway.

The sound of the door closing had her coming back around the corner to find him standing in the doorway. She didn't turn the lights on; there was enough light coming in from the sliding glass door to highlight him.

With her heart pounding in her ears, Bethany squeezed her hands into fists in an effort to ease some of the tension filling her limbs. She moved to stand in front of him and placed her palm on his chest again. "I've never done this before, taken someone home from the bar." She smoothed her palm down to his abs. "But also, had it like this…like it is right now, this give and take of control between us."

It was a raw confession, one without fully naming the D/s play beginning between them. But nonetheless, an admission that could extinguish the dynamic of the power exchange between them. She hoped it wouldn't, but if it did, then at least she could end things now.

There would be no point in going forward with him, even for the sake of good sex, if it wasn't on her terms. Bethany needed to establish the foundation for the both of them.

He nodded. "That makes two of us. I just know that I don't want it to stop."

Relief at his agreement spilled through Bethany, and she smiled, almost ready to giggle. The inexperienced Mistress and her submissive? There was a fabulous book title. Good grief. She shook her head. "Okay, so this is new for both of us.

We can make it up as we go along, or would you feel better if we had rules?"

"Rules? I mean—" He chuckled. "You talking some sort of contract or something because I think that'd be a bit much."

Bethany blurted a laugh. "I thought you've never done this before?"

He rolled his eyes. "I haven't, but that don't mean I don't know what 'this' is that we're doing."

"So I guess we're even." She smiled, gazing up at him. Bethany slid her hand to the back of his neck and moved up on tiptoe. Her lips were a bare breath from his. If he bent only an inch more, they'd be touching. "Colby, would you like to touch me?"

He drew in a sharp breath. "More than I want to breathe, ma'am. Please, may I touch you?"

God help her, she couldn't wait any longer. She wanted to draw it out, make him beg a little more, but there would be time for that later. "You may."

Her words were a breath of a whisper, and less than a heartbeat after they'd left her lips, his mouth was on hers in a hard, desperate kiss. Colby's tongue drove between her lips, stroking and rubbing against hers. At the same time, his hands landed on her backside, and he lifted her off her feet.

Breaking from his mouth, Bethany gulped in a breath as she tilted her head in the other direction and went back for more. She wrapped her legs around his waist and moaned when she felt the thick line of his erection against her core.

Bethany rocked her hips, rubbing herself against him as her tongue stroked over his, and she bit at his bottom lip. Heat exploded over her skin, her pussy clenched, and she clawed at his back, tugging at his shirt. She needed more, needed his naked skin.

Colby spun them, and her back hit the door with a thud. He let her lips go and moved to her throat, sucking and kissing at the tender area below her ear as he rocked his hips forward, rubbing his hard thickness against her denim-covered pussy. With one hand, he held her hair in a tight grip and had the other locked onto one ass cheek—

Grinding—*oh, God!* A high-pitched moan escaped as Bethany's first orgasm rocketed through her fast and hard… and she lost her ever-loving mind.

CHAPTER FOUR

"That was the sweetest sound I think I've ever heard." Rig nuzzled the soft skin of Bethany's neck as she sucked in breath after breath, coming down from the orgasm he'd given her.

The swollen head of his cock was leaking inside his boxers, aching to be balls deep inside her. But she hadn't asked him for that yet. Good thing he was patient because the chance to make her make those sweet sounds again was worth the wait.

She ran her palm up the back of his neck. "I liked making it for you." Her beautiful lips arched into a sated smile, and she slid her hand around and cupped his cheek. "It's time to put me down."

"Yes, ma'am." Rig nodded, did as she asked and then took a couple steps back to give her some space.

Bethany ran her hands over her mussed hair, then pulled the pins from the back, letting the rest of the length spill down around her shoulders. "I want you to always address me in that way. As ma'am. But especially when I give you a direction or command. Is that clear?"

Rig's dick throbbed, more pre-cum oozing from the tip. "Yes, ma'am."

"That makes rule number one, then." She nodded. "Rule number two. If I do something you absolutely do not care for or cannot tolerate, then you should tell me. Immediately. There doesn't have to be a safe word. You can trust I'll respect your boundaries. But—" She held up one finger. "I also need you to trust that I won't make you do something I think you can't handle, and that might mean I push you past a boundary or fear in order to show you how strong you are. Is that clear?"

Rig regarded the expression on her face. Bethany was utterly in control and completely serious. Jesus, she was amazing. The little girl-next-door look about her was like a ruse. Hiding beneath that innocent exterior was a complete and total female Dominant.

Rig never would've thought he'd be in a situation like this or want someone like her. But here he was, staring straight into her big brown eyes, and he couldn't imagine denying her one damn thing.

Although he guessed there might be a few things he wouldn't be into. Pain play being one thing he wasn't sure he'd care for, or letting her peg him in the ass with a dildo or strap-on might for sure be off limits.

Yet for her? Maybe…just maybe, he'd do both and more.

Either way, if she needed to make these rules for him—for them—then so be it. He smiled. "Very clear, ma'am."

"Good boy." As she moved past him into the kitchen, she stroked her palm across his cheek. "Please go to my bedroom, remove all your clothes, and stand in the middle of the room. Link your hands behind your back and wait for me."

"Yes, ma'am." Rig turned and headed into her bedroom. Her brief touch of his face had been both titillating and caring, stirring two different kinds of feelings inside his mind and body. In the very short time they'd spent together, there was already a tenderness building between them that Rig knew shouldn't be there. Yet, it was there nonetheless.

She didn't know him, and he didn't know her, but none of that mattered. The knowledge that she cared about him, would care about him going forward, was as clear in his heart and mind as an Arizona summer sky.

Even if they never saw each other again after the night was over, she'd made a space for him in her heart. How could Rig not put his faith in her? As he stripped off his clothes and then moved into position on the center of the floor at the foot of her bed, he knew he trusted her implicitly.

Rig could hear her moving around in the living room and then watched as she passed by the bedroom doorway into the semi-adjoining bathroom. When she returned, she wore only a lace halter-style bra and matching lace panties.

Rig's cock jerked at the sight of her perfect body, bouncing against his belly, and he felt the wetness coat his stomach, and then a drop oozed down the tip. "God, you're fucking beautiful."

Bethany reached up and gripped his chin in one hand. Squeezing, she pulled his face down to be eye level with hers. "Did I give you permission to talk?"

Rig's eyes went wide as shock blasted through him. Holy shit, she'd gotten his attention, and right quick. He wasn't sure what to think or how to react to her sudden aggression, but his dick was all for it because he almost came. "No, ma'am, you didn't. Please forgive me."

"That's better. Now, mind your manners, or I'll have to punish you." She released his face and then moved away.

Biting back a moan, Rig looked down at his hard-as-steel cock. Apparently, his prick liked the idea of being punished because another drop of arousal dripped down the head and shaft.

Bethany's bare feet came into view, and Rig looked up to

find her with a bathrobe tie in her hands. "I wasn't prepared for you. Next time, I will be. So this will have to do for now."

Next time… God, he wanted a next time. Clearing his throat, Rig nodded his acknowledgment since she hadn't asked him a direct question, nor had she given him liberty to speak.

She moved around him until he couldn't see her anymore, but then he felt her warm hands at his lower back. Her touch rippled through him, stoking his lust higher as she handled each wrist, binding them together with the long strip of silky material.

He wanted to touch her, pleasure her body with his hands, fingers, tongue and cock. But this binding of his wrists took the option away from him. Disappointment warred with excited anticipation, and again, the head of his dick oozed more fluid.

Having his hands tied behind his back might cause some discomfort in his shoulder, but he'd deal with it. The soreness tomorrow would be worth it. After all, his cock had never been this hard in his life, and how he hadn't spurted his release everywhere with what she'd done so far to him was amazing.

"I'm going to touch you. Where I want, and however I want." She moved in front of him, trailing her fingertips along his ass and hip. "It's okay to show your pleasure, to express it with moans and such. I want you to. But no talking unless I ask you a direct question. Is that clear?"

"Yes, ma'am."

"Ooh," she crooned, her lips pursing. "Such a good boy." Bethany wrapped her petite hand around his thick shaft, and Rig sucked in a harsh breath. "You have a gorgeous cock, Colby." She stroked him, once, twice, then pressed the pad of her thumb against the opening at the head. "You want to come, don't you?"

Fuck, her hands on him shot bolts of pleasure up and

down his spine. He shook his head, panting. "No, ma'am. I don't want to come until you do."

She resumed stroking his shaft. "But I came earlier."

"But I—" His cock jerked, ready to orgasm, and he spurted a small stream onto her fingers. Rig gritted his teeth and groaned. Bethany continued, using it to lube his length further. "Fuck!" He tried to pull away, attempting to stop the climax, but she tightened her grip, halting his movement. "Oh Fuck! God, Bethany!"

"Shh. Shh, now. Easy. Breathe." Bethany slid her fist higher to the crown and squeezed. Not hard enough to hurt him, but tight enough to help him beat back his orgasm. "Focus on my eyes and my voice, and breathe, Colby."

Rig did as she asked, and somehow, he managed to push his climax back down. After a few more deep breaths, she slid her hand back down, fisting his shaft again and holding him at the root. "Finish what you were saying."

Lust swamped all of his senses, and Rig swallowed, trying to calm himself further. "I need you to come more than once before I know I've pleased you enough. Your pleasure is all that matters, ma'am."

"Fair enough, but I'll remind you that I own *your* pleasure, and I also own when you give me mine. If I want this pretty cock of yours to come for me, then it will happen. Whether you like it or not." Bethany rose on tiptoe and licked his bottom lip. "Is that clear, Colby?"

His body trembled as lust-filled endorphins flooded his entire nervous system. "Yes, ma'am."

"Good boy." Bethany took Colby's mouth in a kiss, tangling her tongue with his as she held his cock, and it throbbed in her palm. His dick was silky smooth. Thick, hot and impossibly hard. She could feel the blood pulsing through the large vein traveling the length of the shaft.

She was going to edge him—withhold his orgasm—at least for as long as they could both stand it, because she wanted him mindless. Bethany wanted him begging, and she wanted him completely and totally at her mercy. Then maybe she'd let him go to his knees, and he could eat her cunt until she came. Maybe…

Pulling from his lips, she eased the grip off his shaft and ran her fingers down to his sac. "Do you like your balls played with?"

He was panting but still holding onto his control. "Yes, ma'am."

"Good." She cupped him in her palm, lightly gripping the tender skin and massaging the globes of flesh. "Do you know what edging is?" With the thumb of her free hand, she made little circles around the rim of the head as she played with his balls in the other.

He let out a loud, nearly high-pitched moan before he was able to answer her. "Yes, ma'am."

"Have you ever been edged before or done it to yourself?"

He shook his head, his breathing more labored. "No."

"No, what?" Bethany gripped his balls tight and hard.

"Ma'am! No, ma'am!" He threw his head back and growled.

With a smile, she released her vice grip and gently massaged the tender flesh again. "Much better."

Continuing with the tease of her thumb on his cock-head, Bethany released his balls and moved her hand around to his backside, smoothing her palm down the curve of his ass. Although it was possible he'd engaged in ass-play with past partners, she figured it hadn't been in this sort of setting.

She'd never played with a guy's prostate before, and now was the perfect time to start. Having read about it, she knew to go slow, but no matter what, it was definitely going to happen. Bethany slid her fingers between the cleft of his ass cheeks, and he tensed as she grazed his asshole.

She smiled and raised one eyebrow. "Wherever and however, remember? Relax, Colby. Breathe."

Bethany slid her fist down his shaft, then back to the head, slow and easy, using his pre-cum as lubricant. When he was panting again, she licked two of her fingers and slid them through the cleft of his ass once more and, this time, pressed them against his tight asshole. With his chest rising and falling with each breath, Colby's hot gaze bore into hers, and the muscle near his jawline ticked.

Good God, he was gorgeous like this…giving her the precious gift of his submission. Allowing her to touch him in any way she wished. The power of it swirled through her mind like a tornado, and she felt drunk from the sheer over-whelming effect it had on her body.

With their gazes locked, Bethany massaged his asshole and stroked his thick shaft. His nostrils flared as he moaned and drew in hard breaths with each slide of her hand, and his hips rocked forward in opposition with her movements. "That's it. Mmm. Such a good boy." She licked at his bottom lip. "Fuck my fist."

Another minute or two passed, and Colby cried out as a spurt of semen coated the top of her hand. Immediately, Bethany halted her strokes and gripped the swollen head of his dick tight in her fist. "Hold it, Colby. You can do it, sweet baby."

With his face buried in her neck, his deep groans and growls vibrated through her body and settled in her core. When the desire to orgasm finally passed, Colby raised his face, and the expression in his eyes, a cross between pride and desire, sent another shockwave through Bethany. She was awestruck. "Fuck, you're beautiful!"

Tiptoeing up, Bethany took his mouth in a hard kiss and

began to jack his cock again. The taste of his lips and tongue, the feel of his throbbing flesh in her palm and his hard body at her mercy had Bethany on the verge of her own orgasm. As it was, her panties were soaked through, her inner thighs bearing the evidence of the pleasure he was giving her.

After edging him two more times, Bethany was desperate to come, and she feared she might give in and fuck him until they both exploded. But she managed to rein herself in and, instead, go to her knees before him.

The head of his cock was purple from the need to come and increased blood flow, and she ran the tip of her finger along the edge, teasing him further. "So hard for me. Do you need to come, Colby?"

He licked his lips and gazed down at her. "Yes, ma'am, I do. But only if it pleases you."

"Oh, I think it would please me a great deal." Leaning in, she flicked her tongue out, tasting the bead of semen from his last spurt. "Mmm. So sweet."

Bethany sat back on her heels and gazed up at him. As she slid a hand into her panties and slipped two fingers inside her saturated cunt, Colby's eyes went wide. She let out a moan, rubbed her clit for a moment, then pulled her hand free.

With a smile, she bent forward and took his cock between her lips, sucking him into her wet mouth. At the same time, she found his asshole with her nicely lubricated fingers and pressed them through the tight ring of muscle.

Colby's hips shot forward, burying his dick at the back of her throat. "*Fuuuuuckkk!*"

Pushing her fingers an inch or two deeper, she curled them and found what she hoped like hell was his male G-spot. The nearly mindless-sounding moans coming out of Colby gave her the clue she'd definitely struck home.

Massaging it gently, Bethany drew her mouth off his cock, and then, keeping her lips tight around the rim of the head, she sucked hard. In an erratic rhythm, Colby pumped his hips, moaning and groaning as he panted for air.

Bethany circled one of his legs with her free arm to try and help him keep his balance as his entire body went tight—and the first pulses of his climax, riding up his shaft, vibrated against her tongue.

CHAPTER FIVE

"*Fuuuuuckkk!*" Rig's orgasm rocketed from the base of his spine to the head of his cock, and his entire body seized.

With a sweet moan, Bethany pulled her mouth free and took over with her hand. "Oh yes, baby. Yes! So perfect."

Hot, ropey spurts shot from his prick as his climax paralyzed every muscle in his body and made spots form in front of his eyes. Each time she stroked inside his ass, his cock spurted again, coating the floor in front of him. It was endless…and the most amazing, intense orgasm he'd ever had in his life.

When he was finally spent, Colby hung his head and focused on breathing. The room felt fuzzy as if a fog had settled around the space. His shoulder ached, and exhaustion blanketed him.

Bethany stood and smoothed her hands along his arms, and then cupped his face in her palms. "That was the most beautiful thing I've ever seen in my life. Thank you." She rose up and pressed a soft kiss to his lips. "Turn around so I can untie you, and then you can lie down on the bed."

He said nothing but did as she asked. When his wrists were free, he stretched a bit, trying to get the impending soreness to settle down before he climbed onto the bed. Finding her soft pillows, he covered his face with one and breathed the scent of her in.

A few minutes later, she was back in the room, and he felt a warm cloth brush over his sensitive cock and balls. Pulling the pillow away, he watched her as she cleaned him up. It wasn't something Rig had ever had a woman do for him. The clean-up was his job, especially when it came to cleaning her up.

Maybe she'd let him clean her after she'd allowed him to make her come—guilt spilled through him, coating his insides like glue, and he let out a rough sigh.

He shouldn't have come before her.

She should've let him take care of her first.

That was how it was supposed to be.

"Stop it, Colby." She tossed the cloth toward the closet and then handed him an unopened water bottle he hadn't noticed she'd brought in. "You pleased me. You gave me *exactly* what *I wanted*. Remember? That's how this is supposed to work."

Amazing! She knew everything he'd been thinking as if she lived inside his head. Rig wasn't sure how to feel about that, so he shoved it aside. But it further validated that they definitely had a connection. He didn't need to dig any deeper into it.

Sitting up, he cracked the water bottle open and took a swig. "Yes, I know. It's just…" He shook his head and downed another gulp.

Bethany climbed onto the bed and straddled his hips. "You have permission to speak freely now." She smoothed her warm palms down his shoulders to his forearms, then massaged his wrists. "But you can only touch me how I direct you to, okay?"

He gazed up into her gentle eyes, her sandy brown hair a

beautiful halo around her head in the dim light coming from the hallway. "Yes, ma'am."

She took his lips in a soft, sensuous kiss. Her tongue so sweet, Rig wanted to suck it like a piece of candy. She unhooked her halter bra at the back and slipped the neck over her head.

Pulling from his lips, she cupped her breasts in her palms. "Do you want to touch them? Lick them? Suck them?"

As much as he didn't think it was possible, her mischievous little smile had his cock twitching, ready to come back to life. And also the fact that he was about to touch, lick and suck her petite tits. Spent or not, what guy wouldn't get hard at the prospect of a delectable treat? Rig grinned, probably looking far too much like a kid in a candy store. "Yes, ma'am. I want all of that and more."

A little giggle bubbled out of her. "Let's start with the 'all of that' part first. We'll get to the 'more' later."

Bethany pulled her hands away from her bare breasts, and Rig couldn't help but growl at the sight of her tiny rose-colored nipples pulled tight into hard points. She was amazing. Fucking amazing.

Unable to wait another second, he ran his palms up her back, reveling in the softness of her skin, and pulled her torso forward to his mouth. He ran the tip of his nose along her breastbone, and the scent of her skin filled his lungs.

If she were his only source of oxygen, he'd breathe her in forever.

Rig kissed a path to one nipple and flicked the hard tip with his tongue, then sucked it between his lips. Bethany arched her back, moaning as he nibbled the tight nub. Moving a hand from her back, he teased its mate with the pad of his thumb, grazing it lightly over and over again. God Almighty, Rig wanted to lick and suck every inch of her sweet, creamy body, but for now, he sucked her nipples until his cock was hard again, and she was treating him to her high-pitched moans and grinding her panty-covered cunt against his shaft.

Rig smoothed his big palm from her chest to her stomach. "I love how petite you are."

With another one of those mischievous smiles, she leaned back, propped herself up with her hands on his knees, and gave him full access to her pussy. "And I love how big you are."

Glancing down, Rig could see she'd soaked through her panties, and his mouth watered in anticipation of what all her sweet arousal would taste like coating his lips and tongue. Sliding his hand lower, he rubbed her clit through the wet material. "Need to taste you. May I, please?"

Bethany quirked one brow. Using one arm for balance, she pulled her panties aside, dipped two fingers into her soaked cunt, and then raised her wet fingers to his lips. "Suck them clean."

Fuck yes! Without hesitation, Rig parted his lips and sucked them into his mouth. Closing his eyes, he moaned and slid his tongue along the side of each finger, seeking more of her honey. "So sweet. I knew you'd be sweet."

Urging her backward off his lap, Rig pulled her panties down her thighs and tossed them aside. Kneeling between her spread legs, he took a moment to admire her naked body. She wasn't perfect, but no one body ever was or should be, and it made her even more beautiful in his eyes.

She had a small scar near her belly button. Some stretch marks on the sides of her hips. A small, raised mole on her left side. Her tummy was flat but not toned or muscled—which meant it was nice and soft, the way he preferred. Actually, all of her imperfections were what made *her* perfect in his eyes.

Rig was a big guy, and he liked his women to have a little meat on their bones. Her ass was nice and round, too, another bonus. Since he'd gripped her bottom tight in his palms when they'd arrived earlier, he knew for damn sure it fit his big hands perfectly.

"You like what you see?"

Rig cupped her torso in his hands, framing beneath her breasts, then ran his palms down her sides to her thighs before spreading her legs wider. She had only a small amount of pubic hair, just enough to tickle his nose. Her pussy was pink, her clit so swollen it was protruding from its hood. Rig licked his lips, knowing he was going to suck the taut nub until she exploded for him. "You're perfect."

"Thank you." She spread her labia, pulling more of the hood back and revealing her sopping-wet core. "Is this what you want?"

"Yes, ma'am."

"You've been such a good boy. You've pleased me more than I thought possible." She rubbed her tight clit, and Rig's cock jerked, bouncing against his belly. "And now I want you to show me what you can do with your mouth and tongue."

Bolts of electricity rode up and down his spine. And he knew when she came for him, coating his lips with her sweet orgasm, it was possible he was going to die and go to heaven. Once Rig had something so complete, there was nothing else he'd ever need.

Only her.

"OH! GOD! *YESSSSS!*" Bethany threw her head back as Colby latched onto her throbbing clit and sucked. He'd been eating her pussy forever, fucking her with his tongue and fingers so good she'd pretty much gone mindless and boneless too.

He growled and curled his fingers inside her channel, hitting her G-spot as if he'd been born with a damn map to it in his head. And her body responded instantly—in a way it never had to anyone before him—to every single thing he'd done to her.

Since being on her back with his face buried between her legs, she'd come twice, and that was in addition to the orgasm she had when they'd gotten to her place. Tingles slid along her spine, and her skin tightened as she neared a third climax... but what she wanted instead was his thick cock filling her this time.

Gathering her wits about her, Bethany pushed at his head and scooted away from him. "Stop. Enough. No more."

He looked at her, a confused expression on his face. "You just taste so fucking sweet." He wiped his chin with the back of his hand. "And when you come, you get even sweeter. I've never tasted anything like you before. I'm greedy for more."

"Thank you. That's...sweet of you. No pun intended." Letting out a little laugh, she moved off the bed and grabbed a condom from her nightstand drawer. No one had ever told her that her cunt tasted sweet before. Not that Bethany knew for a fact, but she was pretty sure guys said a lot of things they didn't mean during sex.

Colby's compliment felt sincere to her, though. The praise had silly little butterflies, the ones too many romance books mentioned, floating around her stomach. Something was definitely happening between them because she'd never craved the taste of a man before, but now she was. Bethany couldn't get the salty flavor of his orgasm out of her mouth...and she didn't want to.

She was never one who enjoyed letting a man come in her mouth, but with Colby, his scent, the taste of his dick, and his cum, left her wanting more. "I like that you're greedy. But I'm greedy too, and I want to feel that gorgeous cock of yours buried inside me." Climbing back on the bed, she pulled the condom free of the wrapper and rolled the latex down his thick shaft. Reaching over him, Bethany tossed the pillows off the bed and patted the mattress. "Scoot back so you're resting against the headboard."

"Yes, ma'am."

Ma'am… Bethany's lower belly jumped, and her clit pulsed at the term of respect. No matter how many times he said it, the word had the same effect on her. Practically coming out of her skin with anticipation, she drew in a deep breath, straddled him and then slid her pussy along his shaft. "Mmm… there you are."

With one big hand on her buttocks, he tickled the crevice of her ass, and cupped one breast in the other and sucked her nipple. Bethany couldn't wait anymore. The few strokes along his length had her pussy creaming and her belly unbearably tight with the need to orgasm. Tilting her pelvis slightly—the swollen crown of his dick slipped inside the mouth of her cunt. Bethany gasped and paused to—

Colby groaned and gripped the flesh of her ass cheek hard.

"I want all of you buried in me." Bethany cupped the back of his neck in her palms and focused on his eyes as she slid, inch by decadent inch, slowly down onto his shaft, taking his full length inside her. The walls of her cunt, clenched down, and she blew out a breath, relaxing her muscles to accommodate his thickness. "Can you feel that?"

"Yes, ma'am." The whispered answer feathered over her lips.

She slid up and then took him deep again. "Oh God, yes." Desperate for more of him, Bethany repeated the movement, gliding up his shaft to the crown and reveled in the feel of the rim as it teased the mouth of her cunt. "What is it that you feel, Colby?"

"Perfection." He moved his hand from her breast and threaded his fingers in her hair. "It's fucking perfection, Bethany."

Heat bloomed in her tummy, radiating through her body to her limbs. The feel of his naked skin. The words he whispered. The thick air in the room. Every bit of this moment between them wrapped around Bethany, and she couldn't stop herself from moving on him.

And yes, she agreed, they'd found perfection.

CHAPTER SIX

"You're amazing." Rig gazed into the eyes of the most beautiful creature he'd ever seen. Her long hair, messy and also beautiful, hung around her shoulders, tickling his face when she took his lips in a kiss. She moved on him and moaned his name, squeezing his cock with her tight little cunt as she rode him.

Little tingles climbed up and down his spine, and his dick throbbed every time her pussy clenched down on him. Rig needed to make her come again—needed it more than his last breath. The desire to see her face when she climaxed, to know the pleasure he was giving her, took over all other thought.

His pleasure was her pleasure. And he didn't care if she didn't let him come too. As long as she was happy…that was all that mattered.

"I can't get enough of you." With her hands on his shoulders, she rolled her hips, sliding herself back and forth.

The movement allowed her to grind her clit against the front of his pelvis, giving her all the stimulation she needed. He'd never had a woman move like this on him. Never had a woman who knew how to make sure she got off, no matter what. Even though he wanted to be the one to make her come all on his own, without her assistance…he couldn't argue with her method.

She was, after all, in charge.

With both hands on her delectable ass, Rig enjoyed the flex and play of her butt muscles as she worked her body on his. He squeezed and, following her lead, gave her hips a little assistance.

She moaned and took his mouth in a hard kiss. Rig ran a hand up her back, sliding his palm over her perspiration-covered skin.

His orgasm boiled at the base of his spine, but there was no way he'd blow before her. Plus, the desire to grab her hips and slam her down on his prick, over and over again, fucking her so hard she'd never forget him, helped him ignore the need to come. But he wasn't going to give in to that need either. He'd have to find a way to be patient.

Patient while she rode him to heaven and back, making this dick harder by the second. Patient while he listened to her high-pitched whimpers and moans—which only made him want to hear what other beautiful sounds she'd make.

None of those things were a hardship by any stretch because it was all wonderful and overwhelming and fucking unbelievably amazing. By far the best experience of his life.

At least while he was enduring such sweet torture, he got to be completely drunk on her delectable scent as he tasted her lips and sucked and bit her sweet nipples.

She pulled from his mouth. "You're holding back, aren't you?"

Fuck! How did she know what he was thinking? It was like she could hear inside his head. He was too amazed by her intuition at the moment to think about how vulnerable it made him to her. "Yes, ma'am."

Without breaking her stride, she smiled and tucked a lock of hair behind her ear. "Why?"

He frowned. Was she testing him? "Because you haven't given me permission."

"Permission for what?" She rose up and arched her back. Sticking her ass in the air, she moved in short little bounces, teasing the head of his dick with the mouth of her cunt.

Rig groaned and slid both hands down her back to her backside. "Permission to give you more." He licked the nipple, teasing his lips. "Permission to grab hold of the flesh of your ass and fuck into you so hard you scream my name."

"Like this?" She slammed down on him, and Rig lost his breath on a groan.

He gripped the round flesh of her ass. "Fuck yeah!"

Bethany rose up and slammed back down again. "That hard enough? Or do you need it harder?"

"Fuuuuuckkk!" Rig drew in a deep breath and forced the orgasm climbing up his cock to settle. He wanted it harder, but was sure he wouldn't last if she kept this up.

She gripped his jaw with her slender fingers and tilted his head back. "How hard do you want it, sweet baby?"

His breath slid out of him on a strangled growl as she impaled herself on his cock again, their skin slapping together in lust-filled harmony. Rig gritted his teeth. "As hard as you want to give it to me, ma'am."

"Maybe I want you to beg." Bethany nipped his bottom lip and changed her pace, shifting back to the slow and steady slide of her hips, rocking forward and back. But she reached behind her and cupped his balls in her palm and massaged them. "Maybe I want you to be so mindless with the need to come that you can barely articulate the words."

Panic bubbled, lodging like a bitter taste in the back of his throat. He was going to come. If she didn't stop rubbing his sac and fucking him like she was, he was going to lose his fucking load like a teenage boy watching porn for the first time. "Fuck! Bethany! Please!"

"Your cock is so hard I could just ride you at this nice, leisurely pace. Maybe not let you come at all." Holding onto his shoulders, she threw her head back, rocking her pelvis at an absolutely frustrating pace. "Mmm… All. Night. *Lonnnng.* What do you—"

Something snapped inside Rig. Maybe it was because she was taunting him. Or maybe it was simply because he needed to come because his dick was about to explode. Likely, it was a combination of everything…but either way, he lost all control.

Looping his arms around her tiny waist, Rig jerked away from the headboard and rolled them forward. Bethany let out a giggle-squeal when her back hit the mattress, and in the next instant, he was rutting between her parted thighs like some sort of mindless animal—which was what she wanted, wasn't it?

Fine. It was *exactly* what he wanted, too. He'd give Bethany everything she fucking wanted and more…

With his face buried in the side of her neck, Rig pushed her knees up and apart and fucked her hard and fast, driving as deep as he could into her tight channel. The sound of his hips slapping against her ass sent a bolt of lust through Rig so overwhelming his dick jerked, and he knew he'd spurted a little into the condom. "*Fuuuuuckkk!*"

He'd pound her right through the goddamn mattress if that's what it took to bring them both over the edge.

"COLBY! YES, BABY, YES!" Bethany dug her heels into his back as he shuttled in and out of her. All she could do was hold on, and at the moment, she was more than happy to do that. She'd pushed him, taunted him…and it'd been the right thing. Bethany needed to see how far she could take him before he finally gave in and lost control.

Running her palms down his sweat-slick back, she found his tight, athletic ass and dug her fingers into the flesh. The tension in her lower belly grew, and her clit throbbed, aching for just a little more contact…

Colby rose up from her body, resting his weight on his fists planted in the mattress on each side of her head, and then changed the angle of his hips. The shift lined the head of his dick up with her G-spot, and as he thrust forward, he worked her clit with the front of his pelvis.

He'd paid attention. He knew she needed this in order to come. *Sweet God. Oh, my*— "Yes, baby. Just like that."

Bethany gazed up at him in awe. His lips were drawn in a tight line. The muscle in his jaw ticked. The veins in his neck stood out in sharp relief from his skin. Her gaze traveled lower…the thin patch of hair on his chest was soaked with sweat. His abs were tight, also glistening with sweat, the perfect six-pack muscles, something she saw only on magazine covers.

He was an absolutely beautiful man.

That was Bethany's last thought as her orgasm overtook all thought, all reason, and her body arched in rapture. Too far gone in the sensations swamping her body from her pulsing clit and clenching pussy, she only barely registered the groan that morphed into a growl as Colby's orgasm hit him. But then she felt his climax, too.

His thick cock jerked over and over again inside her, spurting his release inside the condom. With each sharp twitch of his shaft, Bethany's cunt clenched down around him and amplified her own waves of climax. It was endless. It was powerful. It was like nothing she'd ever experienced in her life.

It was…perfection.

CHAPTER SEVEN

"I'LL BE RIGHT BACK." RIG SHIFTED TO BETHANY'S SIDE AND then pushed himself to a sitting position on the edge of the bed. As he did, his shoulder screamed in pain, and he was unable to stifle the grunt that forced its way up and out of his mouth. *Idiot!* He took a moment to rotate his arm and rub the tight muscles and tendons surrounding the damaged joint.

Bethany's warm palm settled on his upper back. "You okay, baby?"

He stiffened and stood as if her touch burned. "Oh, yeah. I'm fine. Wore me out, is all." In an attempt to make light of the situation, he tossed a big smile at her over his shoulder before disappearing into the bathroom.

No reason for her to know how much he was hurting. He'd be fine. A couple of his prescription anti-inflammatories and some heat, he'd be right as rain in the morning. After taking care of the condom, he took the liberty of checking the medicine cabinet and under the sink because what woman didn't have—bingo! Ibu's would hold him over until he got home.

Stepping back out to her bedroom, he found she'd arranged the pillows and bedding back into some semblance of order and was sitting with her knees pulled up to her chest. He paused at the side of the bed. "You okay?"

Bethany patted the spot on the mattress beside her. "Oh, I'm just fine. More worried about you and your shoulder, though."

Rig climbed over her and settled where she'd directed him. "Told you. I'm fine."

As she looked at him, a little wrinkle formed between her brows. Apparently, she wasn't going to settle for the standard "I'm fine" answer. Rig let out a sigh and looked away from her penetrating stare. Didn't it figure, after all the awesome sex, the last thing he wanted was a serious conversation about his damn shoulder injury, which would mean he'd have to talk about football and the mess his life became as a result of it?

It didn't matter one bit that earlier in the night, for reasons he still hadn't figured out, Rig had wanted to tell Bethany the whole boo-hoo story. But now? Now, he only wanted to lie beside her and listen to *her* talk or twirl her hair around his fingers…and maybe get to listen to her breathe as she fell asleep.

He didn't want to go into his past.

Football was ancient history. So was college. He was fine. His shoulder was livable. Life went on—end of story.

She moved on the bed, getting into a kneeling position with her ass resting on her heels so they were face to face. Her expression was serious, and he wasn't sure, but she also looked a little angry. "Rule number three—" She bent close, nose to nose, her lips a mere inch from his. "Do not ever lie to me again. Is that clear?"

Everything inside Rig went still as a statue as he focused on the dark brown of her pupils. And then his mouth was moving before he gave an answer any thought. "Yes, ma'am."

Jesus, she was a lot like his boss, Badger, with the "is that clear" stuff. And also, she was about as alpha as Badger was, too. That was the control she had over him. Not that he thought he couldn't argue with her. He could. Maybe… His yielding was more for the fact that he knew there was no point in trying to argue; hell, thinking about it, maybe he couldn't argue with her after all. Either way, she wasn't wrong. The woman knew he was lying.

He wasn't fine.

But letting all of the "not fine" out from the vault he'd hidden it in was completely fucking terrifying. But more so, the bigger fear was that from the moment he'd met Bethany, all he wanted to do was confide it all in her.

She was strong enough to carry it for him—even if only for a little while. It was the only logical reason why he was suddenly bursting at the seams to fill her in on the details.

But what if she wasn't? What if she thought he was a complete idiot for making the choice he did? Or worse, what if she thought he was a coward?

This wasn't some stupid childhood fairytale. People didn't ride off into the sunset together and live all happily ever after. Especially people like him. How could he open up all of his old wounds to a total stranger on the stupid hunch that she'd heal them? Easy answer: he couldn't.

But Rig had a feeling Bethany was going to pry it out of him regardless of whether or not it was going to hurt. And regardless of the fact that in his mind, he *was* a complete idiot for making the choice he did, but worse, he was, for sure, a fucking coward.

***

"Glad we got that cleared up." She gave him a soft kiss before pulling back and resting on her heels again. Whatever his story was, Colby had it locked up tight, and Bethany intended to find the key. She placed her palm on his shoulder. "Can I get you something for this? Ice? Heat, maybe?"

As if he was embarrassed, or maybe ashamed, Colby cast

his eyes down and swiped at his bottom lip with his thumb. "Heat works best."

"Heating pad okay?"

"Yes, ma'am."

"Okay then. Two sec's." Before hopping off the bed, she bent and pressed her lips to his shoulder. She found the heating pad in her linen closet, grabbed a couple of Ibuprofen for him, along with a few more things. When she got back to the bedroom, she held her palm out. "Take these."

The corner of his lip arched into a slight smirk. "Already took some."

Bethany tilted her head to the side. "Did you now." She pursed her lips. "How many did you take?"

"Just two." He shrugged, then winced.

Her heart fell for how much pain he might be in, as worry filled her stomach like tepid water. She blew out a calming breath and reminded herself that even if he was hurting a bit, he was fine. He was breathing, talking, etcetera. "You can take up to eight hundred milligrams at a time. Assuming you don't have a sensitive stomach, you should be able to handle two more."

He took the pills from her, but instead of taking them as she'd directed, he stared at them in his palm. Giving him a moment to reconsider, Bethany went around to his side of the bed and plugged in the heating pad. "I brought some lavender oil. I'm going to massage you first, then you can use the heating pad."

"Bethany, it's not necessary. Really, it's okay."

"I'm sure you *believe* it's okay, especially since you just agreed that you would *never* lie to me again. So, I have no choice but to assume you believe the lie you're telling yourself and thus me."

Looking up at her, his expression was one of a beaten man, and her heart broke for him. But Bethany knew it wasn't as a result of anything she'd done to him. On the contrary, whatever had beaten him down was like a poison in his system, and she intended to draw it out. "Take the pills, Colby. I won't tell you again. And then scoot forward so I can sit behind you."

"Yes, ma'am."

Relief filled her lungs like a fresh breeze at his obedience, and as he washed the pills down with a gulp of water, a sense of peace rushed in like a warm summer storm. The over-the-counter meds were no cure, but they'd ease his pain a bit, she hoped.

Settling behind him, she began to work the oil into the tight muscles of his shoulder. He moaned and sagged a bit, but relaxed as she continued. "I want to hear about it. And I know you don't want to tell me all of it right now. But you need to tell me some. Okay?"

"Yes, ma'am."

Ma'am… She giggled. "Trying to suck up?"

He glanced over his shoulder, one of his big smiles in place —this one appearing more genuine than the others. "Is it working?"

"I'll never tell." She winked and continued with the massage. "Tell me about the shoulder, Colby."

He let out a deep sigh as if preparing himself…then another, before he finally answered. "I had a full scholarship to ASU. Third year in, my shoulder got wrecked so bad—" He shook his head and blew out another breath. "It ended the season for me. I had surgery, but it's always a gamble. It's rare, but some players come back from it. Especially young ones. I didn't."

"I'm sorry that happened to you. It must've been very painful, physically and emotionally." She shifted and helped him stretch his shoulder.

He groaned but then settled again. "Feels like forever ago. Another life, one I'll never live again."

"Obviously, you stayed in the area. Didn't go back home

to your family. How many people in your life here know this about you?"

"One."

"Only one, other than me?"

"No, ma'am. One, *including* you."

Bethany bit her bottom lip and frowned. "I'm honored you decided to share it with me. But I'm also curious: why did you decide to tell me?"

Keeping his back to Bethany, he placed his palm on top of her hands and stilled her massage. "I don't know that I understand why. You asked, I guess, but more so, it just felt like I needed to."

"I see." There wasn't anything else to say. She was his Dominant. Plain and simple. Obviously, he was deeply devastated over the injury—to the point where he'd kept all of it inside. Bethany wasn't foolish enough to believe she could heal an emotional wound that big, but she hoped she'd relieved a little of the pressure from keeping it bottled up. She pressed a kiss to his hand and then slid from behind him. "Let's get some rest."

After helping arrange the heating pad on his shoulder, she settled beneath the blankets next to him and listened as his breathing changed and he fell asleep.

Colby had lost control with her tonight, and in doing so, he'd given himself over to her. His submission meant the world to Bethany. Whether or not he understood the gravity of his actions, or even if that was the reason he'd opened up and shared his pain with her, she wasn't sure.

Now, it was beyond clear to Bethany what was happening between them. Yes, the sex was out of this world amazing, and some might argue that it couldn't lead to more. Ordinarily, Bethany would agree.

But this was different.

Because Colby was different.

And she was different with him.

Maybe she was crazy or too young to know better. Or maybe she was smart enough to know when she'd found "the one." Without a doubt, Colby Jenkins was her one. In one night, like a missing key had been found, everything clicked into place for her, and all the doorways had opened up. And it was because of him.

Bethany fell asleep beside the man who'd changed her whole world—and thanked God for him. Hope filled her heart in anticipation that the morning would hold a new path for both of them to move forward on.

Together.

CHAPTER EIGHT

RIG WOKE WITH THE FEEL OF BETHANY'S WARM BODY AGAINST
his side. His shoulder had a dull ache in it, and his body felt like he'd been at the gym for hours. After wiping the sleep from his eyes, he shifted to his side as carefully as he could and then slid from the bed.

The sun was barely up, and finding his clothes in the dim light of the morning hour wasn't easy. When he did, he made his way to the bathroom and got dressed. Taking one last peek in her bedroom at her sleeping form, he left her apartment and headed out to his truck.

And he didn't look back. He couldn't.

His night with Bethany would forever be the best night of his life, and at the same time, it was the most frightening emotional experience he'd ever had.

Folding into the front seat of his pick-up, he cranked the engine and let it idle long enough to get the engine warm. They fucked. They talked. They connected. Bethany did things to him he never dreamed he'd be into. He wanted more of her, and Rig cursed himself for it. She fucking owned every part of him—mind and body.

He sure as fuck wasn't going to give her his soul too. But she'd taken some of it anyway with all her questions.

Bethany was dangerous because she'd opened doors inside him that he'd kept closed in order to survive. All the shit about his football injury, how he lost his scholarship? Those skeletons needed to stay in the closet he'd had them locked up in. Christ, he hadn't even told her that he was the one who dropped out of college—even though he could've gotten federal aid and loans to finish his degree.

The worst part was he'd wanted to tell her all of it. He'd wanted to wrap himself up in her warmth and comfort, in her love and strength, and let it all float away. But somehow, he'd stopped himself from walking through that emotional arch to freedom. Instead, he skulked off in the wee hours of the morning like a coward.

He didn't leave his cell number for her, and he hadn't gotten hers. There was no way for her to reach him, and he preferred it like that. A knot lodged itself in his throat, and Rig tried to swallow past it but couldn't.

As he drove away from her apartment complex, a hot ache bloomed in the center of his chest. Why did it feel like he'd walked out on the best thing he'd ever found? As if he were walking away from a chance at something real, something solid? Typical of him. After all, he'd walked away from a promising future once. Why not the chance at love, too? "For fuck's sake!"

Love? The instant kind, even? So totally ridiculous!

The last thing he wanted to give Bethany was his heart, too. She'd taken enough. But Rig had a feeling he'd left his soul *and* his heart in that bed with her anyway.

———

BETHANY ROLLED over and blinked the sleep away in the morning light.

Her bed was empty…

Closing her eyes to the reality she wasn't yet awake enough to face, she smoothed her palm across the mattress over the empty space. Instead of finding Colby's big, warm body, she found only the coolness of the sheet.

At some point in the early morning hours, he'd left.

He'd left her bed.

He'd left her.

Hoping against hope, Bethany tossed the blankets off, pulled on a nightshirt and padded out to the living room. Pushing her hair back from her face, she scanned the coffee table and end tables, too. Nothing…

She blew out a breath, swallowed past the lump lodging itself in her throat and moved into the kitchen. She tried to ignore the lack of any sort of "I miss you already. Here's my number" note on the counter as she hit the start button on the Keurig and popped a K-Cup inside, ready to brew. After placing her mug on the drip tray, Bethany scanned the countertop bar…just in case.

No note. No cell number. No Colby.

All her hope was plain…stupid.

Sipping her coffee, Bethany tried to tell herself it was no big deal. What they shared had been special, regardless of whether or not she ever saw him again. What he'd given her…his submission, his secrets, all of it had been a gift. An incredible gift she'd cherish forever.

Better to have it once than never at all, right?

All her self-talk was every bit of rational and true. And although she'd done a fantastic job convincing her head, her heart wasn't getting the message.

In addition, none of her foolish pep-talking had done a damn thing to soothe the fiery ache in her chest, as if she'd been hit by a sledgehammer. Or the empty pit that took up residence in her stomach, stealing her appetite. It definitely hadn't reduced the lump the size of a boulder in her throat, which, no matter how hard she tried, she couldn't swallow down.

Bethany stepped into the shower…and cried.

Once the water flowed over her hair and face, she couldn't pretend anymore that Colby leaving didn't hurt as much as it did. It fucking killed. The sting of her tears mixed with the hot water. Bethany did her best to convince herself that the feel of them washing away meant she'd be okay when she emerged from the darkness of heartbreak.

So, her first one-night stand had resulted in the greatest night of her life…which just so happened to end in tragedy. Awesome. That's sure as hell not how it worked in all those damn romance books she'd read. A bitter laugh bubbled out of her, and she shook her head. *Good grief.*

She'd be okay. Of course, she'd be okay. Why wouldn't she be? Bethany was young. She was independent. And she had her whole life in front of her. She had to be okay.

But truth be told, Bethany might never be as free and trusting—and dominant—with anyone else in the same way she'd been with Colby. The experience with him may have been out of this world, but taking the same risk with someone else was a double-edged sword she wasn't willing to fall on.

Bethany coughed as the taste of bile filled her mouth. The thought of being with another man had her stomach folding in on itself, and she went to her knees on the shower floor. Bending over her legs, she laid her head down on her knees. As the hot water beat on her back, she focused on breathing through the wave of nausea. In and out. In and out. *God, please? Please…take this from me? It hurts too much.*

When the water ran cold, Bethany got to her feet and stepped out of the shower. She wanted to call a friend, her mother, anyone. But the risk of sounding like some pathetic little clinger who bit off more than she could chew was more than she could bear.

After toweling off, she crawled right back into bed. Grabbing her cell, she called in sick to work and then pulled the covers over her head. Hiding in the safety of her blankets was about all she planned to do for the rest of the day and night.

Casual sex was great, but it wasn't for everyone.

Clearly, it wasn't for Bethany.

CHAPTER NINE

"I said, step the fuck back! Now!" Badger grabbed Rig around the waist and yanked him away from the customer Rig had pinned against the wall by his throat.

"What the hell!" Rig glared at his boss.

Taking him by the arm, Badger walked Rig down the back hall and out the back door of the strip club. "The hell is your problem this week? Never seen you like this."

Rig jerked himself free of Badger's grip and paced in a circle, trying to tamp down the rage still boiling in his veins. After a few moments passed, and Badger had lit a cigarette, Rig stopped his pacing and faced the man. "All good, boss. Sorry. Guy just pissed me off, is all."

Badger grunted and blew out a stream of smoke. "That all, huh?"

"Yeah. Give me a break, all right? That's it." Rig put his hands on his hips, and though he tried not to, he knew his tone sounded defensive.

"Let me ask you something—" Badger dropped his spent cigarette on the ground and smothered it out with his boot. "I look stupid to you?"

Rig knew he was treading on thin ice. Badger was irritated, and Rig was the cause. "No way, boss. Come on now. It won't happen again. You have my word."

"Damn right, it won't. I got no time to be bouncing my bouncers. As it is, now I'm late getting home to Rosie and the baby. I got no time for late either. Whatever's got your panties in a bunch, you best take care of it. I don't care what the hell it is. Just fix it. Tonight. We clear?"

Is that clear… We Clear… Rig winced, his chest clenching at the similarity of words to Bethany's. But then shame blanketed him like a thick fog, and he hung his head.

Badger had been an awesome boss. But more than that, he was a badass who pretty much commanded respect, and not because he hadn't earned it. He had. In spades. The last thing Rig wanted was to damage the good thing he had working at Deuce's Cabaret.

The past week had been a special kind of hell for Rig. Bethany haunted his every waking thought, and when he managed to sleep at all, she occupied his dreams. He tried, for all it was worth, to bury her.

But she wasn't going away, and as a result, he'd become a walking time bomb. He'd lost it on three customers throughout the week, and tonight made the fourth. Badger was over it, and frankly, so was Rig.

He was over not sleeping. He was over being in a bad mood. And he was definitely over depriving himself of the one thing he knew would make it all go away; make it all better. Rig knew what he needed to do.

Drawing in a deep breath, he stepped up to Badger and held out his palm. "We're clear, boss." Badger clasped hands with Rig. "If you don't mind, I'm gonna skip out the rest of the night to go…fix it."

Badger's lips curved into a smirk. "Good luck. Hope she's worth it."

"She is." Rig smiled his first smile since he'd left Bethany's bed and took off for his truck. With only a little over an hour to get showered and be in the parking lot behind The Whiskey Barrel, Rig hauled ass to his small studio apartment.

He'd fucked up big time, but he'd do anything to earn her forgiveness, and hopefully, she'd give him a second chance. Because, like he knew the night he met her, Bethany was right where he was supposed to be.

"NIGHT, CONNIE. HOPE YOU FEEL BETTER." Bethany stepped out into the warm Arizona night and headed around the side of the building toward the back parking lot. The night had been busy, as usual, thank God, because she hardly had any time to think about Colby. Plus, Connie had been extra bitchy, which had served as an awesome distraction, too.

She'd still thought of him, though. Actually, she hadn't stopped thinking about him.

Keeping her eyes on her booted feet, Bethany stuffed her hands in her shorts pockets and made her way through the back alley and into the parking lot.

"Ma'am?"

A bolt of heat shot up Bethany's spine. She jerked her head up and stopped dead in her tracks. He was there. Waiting. For her. The levee of hope broke and filled her chest again, and she tried to hold it back. She did, but it was impossible. She swallowed past the lump in her throat and blinked, trying to ward off the tears threatening to fall. "Wh…what are you doing here, Colby?"

"I fucked up. I made a mistake."

Bethany drew in a deep breath and let it out slowly before walking the few remaining feet separating them. Standing in front of him, she tilted her head back to gaze into his eyes. "What are you saying?"

He cleared his throat and then got down on his knees. Bethany's eyes went wide. What the hell was he doing? Colby linked his arms behind his back and bowed his head. "Take me home with you, Bethany. For however long you'll have me. I'm saying I want another chance. May I please have a second chance?"

"Oh, dear." Tears fell, stinging her cheeks, and she placed her palm on the top of Colby's bowed head. Good grief, this man! What on earth was she going to do with him? How could she turn him away, ever?

She couldn't, and she wouldn't.

Bethany smiled as relief filled her heart, and she felt, for the first time in a week, like she could breathe. Smoothing her hand over his head and then down to his cheek, she cupped his chin and tilted his face up to look into his eyes. "You realize if we do this, I'm going to need to make a few more rules for you?"

Colby's heavenly lips spread into the most beautiful smile yet. "Yes, ma'am. I'm counting on it."

ABOUT THE AUTHOR

Dorothy F. Shaw lives in Arizona, where the weather is hot, and the sunsets are always beautiful. She's a self-proclaimed sex scene snob and is proud of it. When she's not writing, she's thinking about writing.

With her ever-open heart, bright red hair, and many colorful tattoos, she truly lives and loves in Technicolor!

Stripped Bounty

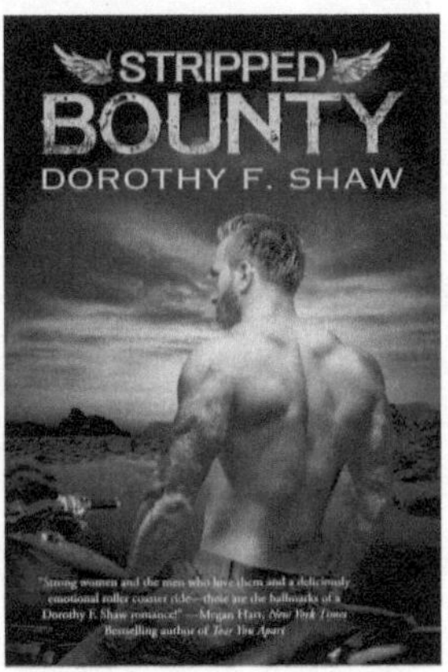

Protecting her isn't an option.
It's a requirement.

Badger finally got Rosie in his bed, but in order to keep her there, he has to figure out how to save her life.

After her drug-running husband gets himself killed, Rosie Santini figures Phoenix is a fine place to get a fresh start. Deuce's strip club isn't too fresh, but the money's easy. As she works the pole, the only gaze she can't ignore belongs to the club's head bouncer, Badger Baxter. But Rosie's seen her fair share of tall, dark, and dangerous, and no way is she heading down that road. Not even for a hot hunk of muscle like Badger.

When he's not bounty hunting, Badger runs security at Deuce's. Rosie should be just another piece of fresh meat in the club's stable of pole jockeys, but all her sexy parts add up to a ride Badger would like to test drive. Trouble is, Badger likes his women submissive, but not broken. She's definitely got baggage he wants no part of. But when her husband's killer shows up looking for stolen cash, she fits naturally under his protection—and it isn't long before she's hooked deep into his heart.

So deep, losing her now would make him bleed in more ways than one.

<u>Warning</u>: *Be on the lookout for D/s sexual play, which may cause drooling and might have you reaching for the nearest man or battery-operated boyfriend.*

<u>Trigger Warning</u>: *This book contains violent situations, including death due to physical altercations and gunfire.*

Turn the page for a sneak peek...

Stripped Bounty

PROLOGUE

The sound of the phone ringing split the silence of the dark bedroom, startling Rosie awake. She rolled beneath the covers and slapped at the nightstand in search of the cordless receiver on its base, missing it a couple of times.

"Fuck…really?" Finally getting a hold of the now torture device and flopping back onto the mattress, Rosie hit "Talk" on the handset and raised it to her ear. "Someone better be dead!"

"Rosie!"

She bolted upright in bed at the urgency in her husband's tone. "Joey? What's wrong?"

"Nuthin'." He coughed. "All good. Listen careful, baby girl." His voice was low and out of breath. "You listenin'?"

Christ, he was always doing that to her—scaring the crap out of her for no damn reason. And he accused her of towing the drama line. Whatever. Rosie swallowed down the panic-induced lump that had risen in her throat and looked at the digital clock on her nightstand. It was after three in the morning. Joey should've been home by then. What the hell had he gotten himself into now? "For the love of… Just get to the point. I'm listening!"

"I took something and hid it. If I don't come home, you need to get it and then, no matter what, you get the fuck out of town."

"What do you mean if you don't come home?" Rosie pushed her hair over her shoulder. "Are you getting arrested again?"

"No. Why do you always assume that? Fuck's sake." He grunted and then coughed again.

Why did she…was he serious? Rosie rolled her eyes. "Do you really want me to answer that question?"

"Whatever. Just listen. Go to the ladies' room at the train station. Under the sink, behind the pipes, you'll find a locker key taped to the wall. Grab it, and go to the self-storage lockers."

"Train station? Which fucking train station? What the hell did you take?" With a shove of the covers, she threw her legs over the side of the bed.

"I took our future, baby."

Good God, she could practically hear the smile behind his words. Rosie looked up at the ceiling, knowing this was going to lead nowhere good. The only place that damn ego of his ever led him was back to jail. Unless... *Oh fuck no.* Cold dread slipped down Rosie's spine, and she shivered. "You rolled the dealer, didn't you? Jesus-fucking-Christ! Are you trying to get us both killed?"

Joey let out a harsh sigh. "Keep your drama ass in check, Rosie! For real. I got this. That small-town fuck has no clue what he's doing. His crew is no better. Trust me, it's gonna be fine. Just take a damn breath for once and do what I say, got it?"

"Do *not* yell at me, *Joey*!" She got to her feet and paced in the small space between their bed and dresser. "You go do something insane, and you expect me to be calm?"

"Yeah, that's exactly what I expect."

Rosie ran her fingers through her hair. She wanted no part of the world of drug trafficking he'd gotten himself into. And she'd made that *very* clear. Not that he ever respected what she wanted or needed. Too busy screwing up to bother. Regardless, Rosie had managed to stay far away from the people he'd been associating with.

What he'd gotten himself into was a one-way ticket to jail or the morgue. Joey had already been to prison one too many times. Jesus, he hadn't even been out more than six months from the last stint. At the rate he was going, it wouldn't be long before he was back behind bars. Or dead.

God, Joey had done a lot of stupid things, made a fuckton more stupid choices, but Rosie never thought he'd do something *this* stupid.

She should've known, though.

Always so goddamn greedy and always wanting more. Joey Santini thought he was a big-time hustler—big enough to pull something this insane off. But he wasn't. He was small-time. Small-town—small fucking potatoes. Especially in the drug world. He was nothing but a runner. A peon. And he'd just put both their lives at risk. She blew out a harsh breath. "Which station, dammit! Where are you?"

"Bridgeport."

Holy shit. That was nearly forty minutes away. The gravity of the situation hit her in the gut like a hard punch. She had no idea what to do. A tear dripped down Rosie's cheek, and she brushed it away. "Are you coming home?"

"I hope so."

CHAPTER ONE

Three months later…

"No Colors or Weapons Allowed."

Rosie Santini read the sign mounted on the brick exterior wall of the establishment. Shaking her head, she opened the solid wood front door and stepped out of the Phoenix hundred-and-four-degree heat and into the dimly lit, air-conditioned strip club.

Back in the day, "colors" meant a biker's patches—as in motorcycle club patches. Commonly found on the back of a leather or denim vest. Considering there was a pack of Harleys parked on the sidewalk out front, Rosie figured in Arizona, that's exactly what the sign referred to. Plus, as she'd learned pretty quickly after arriving in town, barring having a criminal record, people could carry a gun in AZ right out in the open for all to see.

She took a moment as her eyes adjusted, no longer sure if this was such a good idea, and looked around. Type O Negative's "Christian Woman" blared from the speakers as Rosie walked forward on the old green and white—or gray, rather—linoleum-tiled floor. A small birdcage-style stage sat empty off to her left. To her right, the mahogany bar with its large, mirrored backsplash and various bottles of booze stretched along the wall. In the center of the large space sat a collection of small round tables, a tealight candle atop each one, with two pleather chairs arched around them. Doing a quick count, around twenty or so customers occupied the bar. Not uncommon for the middle of the day in a strip club.

Ahead of the tables was the main stage in the shape of an upside-down T. Mirrors lined the back wall with red curtains draped theatre-style at their edges. White rope lights ran along the edges of the narrow stage, leading down to the wide part, which held a pole on each end. There was also a spinning wheel mounted on the ceiling near center stage; she hadn't seen one of those in years. And, finally, another pole near the mirrors along the back wall.

Two girls had the big stage, clad only in their G-strings and stripper heels. One circling a pole, the other on her hands and knees as a patron stood behind her, dollar bill at the ready. Rosie shook her head. Dancers these days barely danced— hardly did anything to put on an actual show or striptease. That was the whole point, wasn't it? At least back in her heyday, it was.

She drew in a deep breath and blew it out. Deuce's Cabaret wasn't seedy…necessarily. But it wasn't plush, either. More that it needed a face-lift. Desperately. Not her first or even eighth choice for employment. But it'd do. At least the music was good.

Rosie circled in place, scanning the corners of the club, looking for cameras. And there wasn't a single one to be found. Anywhere. Hopefully, they had good bouncers. She'd spotted at least two of those throughout the space.

Hiking her big pocketbook a little higher on her shoulder, Rosie blew out a breath and stepped to the bartender. "Hi there."

The big man, clad in a black T-shirt, turned from the cash register and faced her. Rosie lost her breath when she caught sight of his face, but managed to get a grip on herself as he walked toward her. He dipped his chin, cocking his head to the side, as he wiped the bar top directly in front of her with a white bar rag. "You lost?"

Rosie swallowed past the layer of glue that'd suddenly appeared on her tongue. Jesus, he was breathtaking…speechtaking, too. Perfect nose, full lips, the bottom one a tad fuller. Incredible bone structure. Freaking guy could be a model. He was huge, too—muscular and at least six-one, maybe taller. She blinked a few rapid blinks and glanced away from his piercing light-brown gaze.

In an attempt to gain some control of her thoughts, Rosie plopped her pocketbook down on the closest barstool and, after a breath, looked back to him. "No. Not lost. Are you, by chance, hiring?"

He crossed his muscled arms, his biceps bulging, testing the limits of his T-shirt sleeves. "Bar or stage?"

"Bar." She managed a smile.

"Nope." His stare didn't waver, and Rosie took in the small lines around his eyes, but also his strong jaw, partly hidden by a goatee and way-more-than-five o'clock shadow. Yeah, definitely a good-looking man.

"What about waitress?"

"Nope." He dropped his arms and turned his back.

Wow! Had he really just dismissed her like that? *What the hell?* Rosie faced the stage and the dancers again. The Pretty

Reckless's "Make Me Wanna Die" played now. She hadn't been onstage in about two years, and it was the last place she wanted to be again. But she was broke. Getting across the country from Connecticut to Arizona had cost Rosie more than she'd thought. She hadn't anticipated the freaking car dying. Twice. She hadn't anticipated her husband dying, either. *Jerk.* Rosie would never forgive him for putting her in this position.

Biting the edge of her barely existent thumbnail, she turned back around and faced the bartender. Desperate times called for desperate measures. "Okay, fine. Stage?"

With his back still to her, he glanced up from the bottle he was wiping down and caught her gaze through the reflection in the mirror. "You sure about that?"

Was she sure? Rosie'd already been to six other bars that day and three the day before. No, she wasn't fucking sure, but she needed a goddamn job. "Absolutely."

He turned, stepped to the bar top and rested both his hands on the edge. Did a muscle in his jaw just tick? Again he dipped his chin and cocked his head to the side—almost as if he was sizing her up and judging her abilities right there on the spot.

A beat of nervous energy rolled through her. Talk about feeling like a bug under a microscope. Jesus, she was uncomfortable. Rosie crossed her arms and jutted out her chin. The guy might be hotter than hell, but the last thing Rosie needed was bullshit from some stranger right now. "What?"

He pursed his lips, his firm gaze steady on her for another few moments before rubbing his palm along the side of his whiskered jaw and letting out a sigh. "Far side of the stage. Follow the hall to the back. Evie'll help you out."

"Oh." She cleared her throat. "Okay then." Rosie shouldered her bag, feeling a bit like she'd disappointed him. Which was pretty weird, considering she didn't even know him. "Thanks."

Turning on her heel, she stepped away from the bar. He was still staring at her. She knew it. Rosie could feel his gaze like a physical touch, skittering down her spine and over her skin as she made her way across the club in the direction he'd sent her. The screwed-up thing was, rather than creepy, the feel of his eyes on her was titillating.

Considering she'd only lost her husband three months ago, her body's reaction made her feel even more uncomfortable than she'd felt standing in front of him. Shrugging all of it off, Rosie walked through the narrow doorway in the far corner of the bar and down the empty, almost sterile hall.

And back into a world she hadn't wanted to ever visit again.

Badger shook his head as he watched the tall, slender brunette with the sad, dark-brown eyes walk toward the back hall. "Shame."

"What's that, Badge?" Deuce came up to the bar.

Badger glanced over to him. "Fresh meat."

The owner took a seat in his spot at the end of the bar. "Fresh meat's always good in my book. Nothing shameful about that."

Badger grunted and reached for a fresh glass. "You want something?"

"Eh, just a seltzer water. Evie's been nagging me about soda." Deuce clasped his hands together on the bar top and looked toward the stage.

Badger filled the glass with the clear carbonated fluid. "Hate to break it to you, boss. But this is soda."

"Like hell it is. It's water with bubbles in it. Smart ass. Now, grab me a lemon."

Badger chuckled and placed a lemon wedge on the edge of the glass. "We're fresh out of umbrellas."

"Kiss my ass." Deuce chuckled and sipped the drink.

"Maybe later." Badger grabbed the clipboard from the side of the register and went back to taking inventory.

Didn't matter what the boss said. Pretty girl like that one ending up being another stripper was a damn fucking shame. No two ways about it.

For a minute, since she'd asked about tending bar or waitressing, Badger thought, or maybe hoped, she might not be another pole jockey. So much for that. She had to have been on stage before. Sadly, you could take the girl out of the strip club, but you couldn't take the stripper out of the girl. Eventually, they came back. Especially if they still had some looks and a body. This one had both…in spades. Her eyes had gotten to him, though.

Badger looked up from the beer cooler to see her walking back across the bar toward the exit. She glanced over at him but quickly looked away before stepping out into the bright Arizona sun. Yeah, eyes were always a weakness or a warning for him. Hers were sad, like she'd seen some hurt in her days. But they were skittish, too. The skittish smacked of more than hurt in her past.

Regardless, he didn't mess with the strippers anymore. Those days were long gone. But even if she hadn't turned out to be a dancer, Badger would've steered clear anyway. There was enough "more" behind those sad and skittish eyes of hers for Badger to keep his distance. He didn't need the drama or the headache that came along with that amount of luggage.

The front door opened again, and the weekday bartender, Wendy, walked in. "Hey, Badger." She waved as she passed by him on her way to the office as if she wasn't over thirty minutes late for her shift.

"You're late, and I got shit to do besides cover your ass behind the bar."

She spun around, facing him, and shrugged, arms out at

her sides. "Sorry. I had a flat." She continued walking backward before turning again and disappearing down the hall.

Badger grunted before staring down at the clipboard in his hands again. Damn bar staff were just as bad as the dancers. It wouldn't matter so much if he wasn't always the one on point to cover until they brought their asses in. He was supposed to just run security, not the bar staff, too, but the lines tended to blur. Mostly because Badger had a tendency to blur them.

Not that he'd admit that to Deuce if his life depended on it.

"You got some bounty hunter work to attend to?"

He glanced over at Deuce and nodded. "Yeah. Got a lead this morning on a skip I've been tracking."

His boss looked at his watch. "Good luck. See you back here 'round eight?"

"'Course." He set the clipboard down and jerked his chin at Deuce as he stepped out from behind the bar. "Earlier if I can. Order's ready to go. Don't wait up, honey."

"But, darling, we haven't had any quality time together."

"Yeah, yeah." With a wave over his shoulder, Badger chuckled and headed for the same hall he'd sent the brunette down. As he passed the dressing room, he gave a nod to Evie, Deuce's old lady. After a quick stop in the office to grab his gun, he stepped out into the daylight, lit a cigarette, and made his way to his pickup.

It was time to give his other career a little attention.

Want more?
Head to my site to find all links to my available backlist:
www.DorothyFShaw.com

Available from all major e-sellers in digital and print.

This book is a work of fiction. The names, characters, places, and incidents are products of the writer's imagination or have been used fictitiously and are not to be construed as real. Any resemblance to persons, living or dead, actual events, locale or organizations is entirely coincidental.

Dorothy F. Shaw
Phoenix, Arizona
A FEW MORE RULES
Copyright © 2017 by Dorothy F. Shaw
ISBN-13: 978-0-9978310-6-1
ISBN-10: 0-9978310-6-5
Draft2Digital ISBN-13: 978-04638732-1-2
Edited by: Tera Cuskaden
Cover by: Damn Women Promotions - Sidda Lee Rain

Red Queen Publications electronic publication: August 2017

Publishing History
Digital/Print 1.0 editions /August 2017

Red Queen
Publications